Teens and Bullying

Teens and Bullying

Gail B. Stewart

TEEN *Choices*

ReferencePoint Press®

San Diego, CA

© 2016 ReferencePoint Press, Inc.
Printed in the United States

For more information, contact:
ReferencePoint Press, Inc.
PO Box 27779
San Diego, CA 92198
www. ReferencePointPress.com

LIBRARY OF CONGRESS CATALOGING-IN-PUBLICATION DATA

Stewart, Gail B. (Gail Barbara), 1949-
  Teens and bullying / by Gail B. Stewart.
    pages cm. -- (Teen choices)
  Includes bibliographical references and index.
  ISBN-13: 978-1-60152-908-4 (hardback)
  ISBN-10: 1-60152-908-2 (hardback)
  1. Bullying--Juvenile literature. 2. Bullying--Prevention--Juvenile literature. 3. Aggressiveness in adolescence--Juvenile literature. I. Title.
  BF637.B85S756 2016
  302.34'30835--dc23
                                                                                2015000449

Contents

A Hurtful Choice

Kaitlin, now eighteen and a freshman in college, still has difficulty talking about the bullying she endured as a middle school student without crying. It was the worst experience of her life, she says. It began the moment she was first confronted by two girls in her seventh-grade homeroom, and it continued for nearly two years.

She was new to the school, having recently moved from a rural town in central Wisconsin to a southwest suburb of Chicago. Being in a new school and not yet knowing anyone did not worry Kaitlin. In fact, she remembers, she was looking forward to making friends with her new classmates:

> I didn't know anyone before school started. It's odd looking back because I wasn't really nervous about starting a new school. I'd always had a pretty easy time making friends back in my old school in Wisconsin. My mom was always calling me a "people person" because I love getting to know new people. I'm hardly ever shy, and I like having fun. But there weren't any girls my age in my new neighborhood, so I didn't really know anybody yet. I just assumed I'd just meet them on the first day of school—I was actually really excited about it.[1]

Targeted

Her first few days at the new school were far from easy. Two of the girls in her class approached her and asked if all girls from Wisconsin dressed like she did. Another inquired if she was unpopular in her old school. And in the hallway between classes, two boys came up to her and asked if her whole family lived in a barn back in Wisconsin. Some of her classmates chose to join in, making animal noises, like mooing and oinking. Others fanned their noses, as if Kaitlin smelled bad. And as many of her classmates laughed heartily, Kaitlin felt sad and alone.

She says that even now—more than six years later—she still remembers the humiliation she felt at being rejected by people who did not know her:

> I remember lying on my bed and crying when I got home from school. I was trying to figure out what I had done to deserve what they were doing to me. I didn't really dress any different than the rest of the girls. I was sure I hadn't been rude to any of them. But they were so rude to me! Whenever the teacher would call on me, the other kids were snickering, like I was talking in a foreign language or something. All I knew was that I just felt so lonesome for my friends back home [in Wisconsin].[2]

By the end of that first week Kaitlin felt nervous and frightened. She woke up every morning with an upset stomach and could hardly eat breakfast because she was thinking about what lay ahead. She knew the mean questions and animal noises would start the minute she got on the bus. And she had no idea what she should say or do to make the bullying stop.

> "I remember lying on my bed and crying when I got home from school."[2]
>
> —Kaitlin, a college student who was bullied during middle and high school.

What Is Bullying?

Bullying is the term most commonly used for the abuse Kaitlin suffered during middle school. Bullying is commonly defined as unwanted, aggressive behavior—often among school-aged children or teens—that involves a real or perceived

Bullying is often a repeated behavior that leaves victims feeling dread and insecurity. Some victims suffer physical and mental distress that can lead to depression or thoughts of suicide.

power imbalance. Bullying is almost never a one-time event and is usually repeated over time.

This abuse can take many forms—from shoving or tripping someone to name-calling and taunting. Bullying can also consist of spreading rumors about someone. And many bullies use cellphones or computers to post embarrassing photographs or cruel messages about someone else to a wide audience on social media sites.

Psychologists know that bullying is very common, especially in schools. According to StopBullying.gov, a website managed by the US Department of Health and Human Services, approximately 25 to 33 percent of American students report that they have been bullied at school. Most of the bullying occurs during the middle school years, but in some cases it can continue even through high school.

Bullying Has Risks

Youth guidance counselor Anna Mann says that when teens make the choice to participate in bullying behavior, they are taking part in a highly risky situation. She says that being bullied can cause great emotional harm and can lead to depression, anxiety, substance abuse, and, in some cases, suicidal thoughts. "This isn't just kids being kids," she says, adding,

> Bullying is not good-hearted kidding around among friends, where everyone understands that the words aren't meant to be serious or mean. Bullying is harassment, and it is meant to hurt or isolate someone else. When young people make the decision to bully someone, they're engaging in behavior that can be extremely hurtful and can even have terrible, irrevocable consequences.[3]

Teachers, counselors, and other professionals who work with young people understand that the teenage years are full of challenges and difficult choices. Whether to bully, or how to respond when others engage in this behavior, is a choice that many of today's young people may have to make. And that decision may have lasting effects for all involved.

Chapter One

The Faces of Bullying

Bullying has existed for centuries—as long as there have been people using words or physical means to humiliate and harass others. In some cases it was the school yard bully beating up a younger or smaller classmate to steal his lunch money; in others, it was a group of girls whispering among themselves as they made fun of a classmate who was overweight or whose clothes were not as fashionable as their own.

But even though bullying is not a recent phenomenon, research about the causes and effects of bullying is surprisingly new. In fact, the first psychological study of bullying was not initiated until the 1970s. Dan Olweus, a Swedish graduate student who had recently completed his doctorate at Norway's University of Bergen, long had been fascinated by the aggression used by some schoolchildren to intimidate their peers. He was curious about what motivated them to engage in bullying behavior, and he wondered why certain people were targeted as victims while others seemed to escape the bullies' fists and cruel words. At that time few psychologists thought bullying was a topic that warranted scholarly attention, but Olweus was determined to understand the dynamics of bullying among young people.

The Earliest Bully Research

Olweus collected as much information as he could about bullies and those whom they targeted. He began by interviewing one thousand sixth- and eighth-grade boys in schools throughout Stockholm, Sweden's capital. He asked the boys to name classmates who were known as fight starters or bullies. He asked for details about how those boys behaved and the types of aggression they inflicted on their classmates.

After contacting the boys who had been named as bullies, Olweus received permission to perform a number of psychological tests on them. He even visited their homes and talked with the bullies' parents about how their sons had been raised. Were the parents well educated? How did they discipline their sons? Olweus also spent time interviewing the boys' teachers to see if the size of the class or the scholastic abilities of the boys seemed to be a factor in bullying.

The research Olweus did in the 1970s laid the groundwork for other psychologists to discover what it was that set bullying apart from other forms of cruelty and abuse. Through his research Olweus determined that for behavior to be termed *bullying* it had to satisfy three criteria: The first was that the behavior had to be either verbal or physical aggression or a combination of the two. (Cyberbullying, which did not exist at the time, was added later.) Second, the behavior had to be repeated over time rather than just a one-time confrontation. The third criterion, Olweus stated, was that true bullying had to involve a sizable gap in power between the bully and the victim. He noted, "A special thing about bullying types is that kids do it even when the victim seems helpless."[4]

Physical Bullying

Since Olweus's early research, psychologists around the world have added their own research and observations to try to understand how and why bullying occurs. There was no doubt that bullying took various forms, and all could be tremendously hurtful. The oldest form is likely physical abuse, such as tripping, hitting, pinching, or other means to injure and thereby belittle a victim.

New York piano instructor Sylvia Hall remembers being bullied as a sixth-grader nearly forty years ago by classmates who threw spitballs and bits of eraser at the back of her head. "I

Bullying can take many forms in school. The most common are physical harassment such as shoving or tripping victims in hallways. In classrooms, victims might suffer humiliation by becoming the target of thrown or flicked objects.

was new to the school, but I had no idea why so many of the kids didn't like me," she says.

> It still is humiliating to talk about. I just sat there at my desk, and I could hear kids—mostly boys—tearing off bits of paper from their notebooks, and I'd just kind of brace myself, knowing was going to happen. Back then I wore braids, and the back of my neck was exposed. I'd come home with little red spots on my neck from getting hit with those pieces of eraser. That hurt more than the spitballs, but it was all really embarrassing because most of the kids were laughing. And the teacher had no idea at all that it was happening because they did it while she was writing on the blackboard, so she was clueless. And no, I didn't tell her—that would have made it worse.[5]

Sometimes physical bullying can be far more severe. In her book *We Want You to Know: Kids Talk About Bullying,* researcher Deborah Ellis includes an interview with Cory, who was small for his age in eighth grade when he was routinely physically bullied by a group of bigger boys on the school playground:

> They surrounded me and tried to grab me. They said they wanted to airplane me—you know, throw me through the air. I curled up in a fetal position to try to protect myself, and I was kicking out at them and yelling at them, but there were a lot of them. They grabbed me by my feet and swung me across the schoolyard. My whole back was cut up from skidding across the yard. They picked me up and just threw me.[6]

In addition to the fear and physical pain experienced by victims of such bullying, many say the emotional pain is often even worse. Being pushed around in front of their classmates or friends is extremely humiliating. "When you're getting shoved or beat up by other guys in the hallways, it's more than embarrassing," says Bill, a seventh-grader who lost a tooth in 2012 when a classmate shoved his face against a bank of metal lockers. "You don't want to get mad or even show you're mad, because they'll just do it more. And you just look even weaker in front of your friends, and that's no good."[7]

> "They grabbed me by my feet and swung me across the schoolyard."[6]
>
> —*Cory, a fifteen-year-old, remembering when he was bullied in eighth grade.*

Vulnerable Targets

According to the antibullying website Just Say YES, twice as many instances of physical bullying are committed by boys than by girls. And while their targets are usually other boys, there have been many cases in which girls are singled out for physical bullying too. "All it takes to be physically bullied is to be different somehow," says counselor Anna Mann. "It may be a disability that makes the victim look like an easy target, or maybe a person who is perceived as different in some other way—a different religion or ethnicity, or gay, for example. Besides that, the target is perceived as physically weaker and less likely to be able to fight back."[8]

Gabrielle Ford is one example of a student who was relentlessly bullied because of her physical disability. When she was thirteen, Gabrielle was diagnosed with a rare neuromuscular disease called Friedreich's ataxia. The disease would eventually confine her to a wheelchair, but in its earliest stages her legs became very weak and she needed to use leg braces to walk. Because she stumbled and lost her balance easily, she soon found herself the target of laughing bullies as she walked through the school halls and especially when navigating stairs. "I didn't always fall down by myself," Gabrielle recalls. "Kids loved to step on the backs of my heels to throw me off balance. Someone would push me from behind to watch me stumble, or shove me into another kid, laughing. My books would be knocked from my hands, and someone might kick them for fun and watch as I scrambled after them."[9] And to add more misery to her school days, some classmates would mock her lack of balance by calling out things like "Are you drunk?" or "You really ought to lay off the booze, Gabe!"[10]

Verbal Bullying

The second type of conventional bullying is verbal—calling people names or making rude remarks about them as a way of humiliating them. Although statistically boys are responsible for approximately twice the amount of physical bullying as girls are, boys and girls do an equal amount of verbal bullying. Millions of young people are targeted for verbal bullying each day in the United States, and many would attest that those words can be every bit as painful as a physical attack. "That old rhyme, 'Sticks and stones can break my bones but names will never hurt me' is so completely false," says Amy Schultz, a

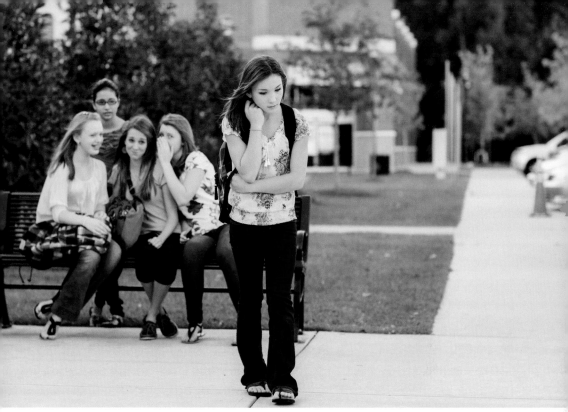

Name-calling and harassing victims with rude or hateful remarks is another common form of bullying on school grounds. While teachers and administrators might witness and intercede in a physical incident of bullying, verbal abuses are more difficult to detect and stop.

graduate student in psychology who admits that during middle school she was part of a group of girls who bullied classmates regularly. "Every once in a while, I think back on those years, and I can actually feel my face get red with shame," she says. "My friends and I didn't even take a minute to think that we were causing such pain among the girls we picked on. But to us, it was just funny—just a way of making each other laugh."[11]

Schultz says her group of friends did not physically hurt anyone, but they did plenty of name-calling and laughing:

> We all thought we were pretty witty and clever, thinking up funny nicknames for the girls we enjoyed bullying. But now looking back, I'm so sorry I got into that stuff. I can still see the looks on the faces of some of those girls and how embarrassed they were when we'd make fun of their looks, their weight, the clothes they wore, whatever. It was

terrible, and I know that now. Actually, I take that back. Deep down, I *did* know it was very wrong back then, but I either wasn't smart enough or mature enough to stop.[12]

Social Bullying

Another type of bullying is known as social bullying, and it often involves spreading rumors about others in order to humiliate them. Other times, social bullying takes the form of intentionally leaving someone out so that they are isolated from the rest of a group. One of the cruelest types of social bullying is to publicly embarrass someone. This happened to one high school boy who was interviewed by researcher Ellis. The teen, who asked not to be identified, had been born with a mild form of cerebral palsy. He was clumsy as a result of the disease, and in elementary school he was often teased and bullied on the playground. By the time he was in high school, he was used to being mocked and pushed around by other boys.

However, he says, the meanest thing that ever happened to him in high school was being socially bullied by a girl who invited him to a school dance. He remembers how excited he was to be included at last. "I thought, finally, all this [bullying and teasing] is over and I'm going to have friends! She bragged about it all over the school, about how she and I were going to the dance together."[13]

The night of the dance, with a new suit and a haircut, he was dropped off at the school by his mother, and he waited excitedly by the door for his date to arrive. However, when she walked in, she was with another boy. "[She] says to me, really loud so everyone could hear, 'I can't believe you thought I would go out with you!'" he remembers. "And she started to laugh and tell

> "Deep down, I *did* know it was very wrong back then, but I either wasn't smart enough or mature enough to stop."[12]
>
> —Amy Schultz, a graduate student, recalling her own bullying behavior in middle school.

Gabe and Izzy

Gabrielle Ford, a girl with a progressive neurological disease who became a target for bullies in middle school and high school. After high school, she sank into a deep depression and felt more and more isolated from friends and former classmates. It was then that Gabe decided she wanted a dog. Her mother agreed, and Gabe adopted a coonhound named Izzy, who became her best friend and constant companion.

But it was not until Izzy became ill with a neurological condition that was eerily similar to her own that Gabe found the strength to become more active and vocal about getting her dog the care she needed to survive. As a result, she was invited to appear on *Animal Planet* to talk about her bond with Izzy as well as the bullying she endured. That led to invitations to come to schools and talk about her experiences as a victim of bullies. And although Gabe was not confident about speaking publicly, she found that students were very receptive, and it helped to have Izzy with her.

"Time after time kids shared with me how they had been bullied," Gabe says. "For these students, it's almost as if someone has finally come to save them. Simply to hear someone talking openly about bullying makes them feel they've already been rescued."

Gabrielle Ford with Sarah Thomson, *Gabe & Izzy: Standing Up for America's Bullied.* New York: Dial, 2014, p. 121.

everyone what a loser I was. The guy who was her date hadn't known anything about this. He even apologized to me."[14]

It was, he says, the most humiliating experience of his life, but he was too embarrassed to call his mother for a ride home. "For four hours, I stayed at the dance, with folks laughing at me and pointing at me. I pretended it didn't bother me. When Mom picked me up [after the dance] and I got into the van and closed the door, that's when I started to cry."[15]

Cyberbullying

Most of Dan Olweus's findings about bullying remain as applicable in the twenty-first century as in the 1970s. But since that time one new form of bullying has captured public attention like no other before it. Known as cyberbullying, it involves the use of electronic technology such as a cellphone or a computer to spread rumors, send unflattering photos, and post any other information online that will embarrass or humiliate someone else.

In a great many cases, bullies use Facebook, YouTube, Tumblr, MySpace, Twitter, or other social networking sites to ensure that their harassing and humiliating posts reach a large number of people. According to the i-Safe Foundation—dedicated to ensuring the safety of young Internet users—more than 25 percent of teens and adolescents say they have been cyberbullied. In another study of Internet behavior of high school seniors (this one headed by Catherine D. Marcum, professor of justice studies at Appalachian State University), 31 percent say they have been cyberbullied.

Chelsea is a young woman who has experienced cyberbullying firsthand. She became the target of a cyberbully when she was in middle school. A girl in her class started an Expage (the precursor to MySpace and Facebook) devoted to bashing Chelsea. "The title of the page," says Chelsea, "was 'Let's Kick Redhead's Ass.' Redhead meant me. She put everyone's name on the page and got them all to write down what they didn't like about me."[16]

Everybody joined in, even some of Chelsea's friends. Though they later explained to Chelsea they were told the page was just a joke, she was upset by the threats and insults. She felt embarrassed and betrayed—and very alone. "I was devastated," she remembers. "I couldn't believe this bad thing had happened to me. These kids were the kids I had grown up with!"[17]

Cruel and Constant

Psychologists view cyberbullying as an extreme and devastating form of bullying. Unlike verbal and physical bullying, the victim cannot simply walk away from the abuse. The mean texts, e-mails, Tweets, and other messages can continue to arrive long after the school day is over. With people constantly connecting to each other by phone, home is no longer a refuge from the mean-spirited and hurtful comments. Jenna, who was cyberbullied as an seventh-grader, says,

> You absolutely hate hearing the beep that you've got another message coming in. You are torn between wanting to just ignore it because you're pretty sure it's going to be mean, and wanting to check to see if possibly someone is posting something supportive, coming to your defense. You just can't ignore it, and all you think about is how many people are reading all of [those posts.] I remember being so nervous, so stressed out.[18]

Another upsetting aspect of cyberbullying is that by its nature it can be virtually permanent, compared to a shove or a trip in the lunch line or a mean insult yelled by a bully on the playground. The mocking photograph or hateful comments meant to embarrass someone remain as long as the creator of the page wants them to. But while the victims of cyberbullying receive wide-ranging—and completely unwanted—attention, the same cannot be said for the bullies themselves. Some social media sites allow someone opening an account to remain anonymous by using a different screen name so a user cannot be identified.

> "You absolutely hate hearing the beep that you've got another message coming in."[18]
>
> —Jenna, on being cyberbullied in seventh grade.

Perhaps the cruelest aspect of cyberbullying, says bullying researcher Emily Bazelon, is that far more people are witnesses to someone's degradation than would be during a face-to-face bully encounter:

> Because teenagers often have hundreds of Facebook "friends," rumors and slights can rapidly spread in a way that wasn't possible in the era of landlines. Add in friends of friends, as Facebook's privacy settings for teens automatically do, and the audience for a cruel post easily expands into the thousands. The cleverer and more cutting the insult, the more likely it is to go viral.[19]

Learning from Adversity

For years bullying or being bullied was considered just a part of growing up. "My grandpa always tells us kids that the bad stuff that happens to you when you're young makes you stronger as an adult," says thirteen-year-old Patty, who endured several weeks of continuous cyberbullying. "But he doesn't really understand about how kids are on the Internet all the time, with their computers and cellphones and Facebook and all the mean things that kids can do to each other now. He doesn't get what we go through because he never experienced it himself."[20]

Even so, says psychologist and bullying expert Elizabeth Englander, there is some truth in the fact that although parents might prefer to shield their children from bullying, the vast majority of young people do bounce back after a bullying experience. "Children need to encounter some adversity while growing up," she insists. "There's a reason why Mother Nature has promoted the existence of run-of-the-mill social cruelty between children. It's how children get the practice they need to cope successfully with the world as adults."[21]

That said, warns Bazelon, there is a catch to Englander's theory: Some young people do *not* rally after being targeted by a bully. "And we're not very good yet at knowing who will emerge stronger from taunting and who will be seriously harmed by it—or, God forbid, succumb to it," she says. "Meanness that leaves one kid unscathed in the long run can destroy another one."[22]

> "There's a reason why Mother Nature has promoted the existence of run-of-the-mill social cruelty between children."[21]
>
> —Elizabeth Englander, psychologist.

The Unspeakable Outcomes of Bullying

Bullying, no matter what form it takes, is a demeaning experience. But cyberbullying is distinctly different from all other forms of bullying. Texted or posted comments or photos can reach dozens, hundreds, even thousands of people in an instant. And once released into the cyberworld's social media circles, they rarely can be withdrawn. What's more, bullying posts and texts follow their victims home, to school, to work—basically anywhere a teen's daily routine takes him or her. For some teens, the humiliation of this is simply too much to bear.

Rebecca Sedwick, a twelve-year-old from Lakeland, Florida, endured more than a year of bullying at school before her mother learned about it and began homeschooling her. But when the bullies began sending Rebecca online messages that she should kill herself, she became more and more distraught. Finally, unable to stop the bullying, she jumped to her death at an abandoned factory on September 10, 2013.

In 2011 high school freshman Jamey Rodemeyer of Buffalo, New York, also killed himself after being bullied. The fourteen-year-old had come out to his family and classmates as bisexual, and he was an active protester against homophobic bullying

In 2012, Alyssa Rodemeyer cries as she speaks at an antibullying rally in San Francisco. Alyssa's brother, Jamey, took his own life when he suffered threats both verbally and on social media sites after choosing to be open about his bisexuality to his friends and classmates.

Entertaining the Bystanders

Many bullies say that one of the most enjoyable aspects of bullying is receiving the attention and admiration of bystanders. Mark, a sixteen-year-old from La Grange, Illinois, admits that when he was in middle school he verbally bullied other boys while his classmates looked on.

"It was like being on stage," he remembers. "I was kind of known as the class comedian back then, and it was kind of a rush to insult them or make fun of them while my friends watched. It was kind of fun, and I think I was more focused on who was standing around watching than I was on whoever I was making fun of. I really felt like I was on stage. I remember saying put-downs I'd heard on TV, stuff that at the time I thought was hilarious, like 'Your sister's so ugly her picture's on the dog food cans.'

Mark says he would not have kept it up if he had not been getting laughs from the bystanders. "I'm not saying it was their fault," he says. "I'm completely to blame. But really, I'm almost 100 percent positive that if they hadn't been there laughing, I wouldn't have been saying that stuff. I think if they'd just walked away, I would have, too."

Mark, interview with the author, January 4, 2015.

in his school and community. He had also been open about being bullied verbally on the social media site Formspring, receiving such messages as "JAMIE IS STUPID, GAY, FAT ANND [sic] UGLY. HE MUST DIE!" Another read, "I wouldn't care if you died. No one would. So just do it :) It would make everyone WAY more happier!"[23] Soon afterward, Jamey hanged himself.

Tracy Rodemeyer, Jamey's mother, was appalled that the cruelty aimed at her son continued even after his death. She recalls her daughter's experience when she attended a school dance:

She was having a great time, and all of a sudden a Lady Gaga song came on, and they all started chanting for

Jamey, all his friends. Then the bullies that put him into this situation started chanting, "You're better off dead!" and "We're glad you're dead!" and things like that. My daughter came home all upset. It was supposed to be a time for her to . . . have fun with her friends, and it turned into bullying even after he's gone.[24]

For the many children and teens who are repeatedly targeted by bullies, simply navigating through the day can be both agonizing and depressing. One of the challenges is to understand what influences can cause some to bully and to identify who are most at risk of becoming bullies or victims of bullies. And once those factors are clearly understood, perhaps society can find effective ways to stop bullying.

Chapter Two

The Many Competing Influences on Teens

The forces that influence teen behavior are many and varied. Immediate events, societal trends, and the people with whom they interact on a daily basis all have some influence on the choices teens make. A teen's circle of friends, for instance, can influence both good and bad behavior. A recent University of Oregon study "found that middle school students whose friends were prone to misbehave didn't do as well in school as kids whose friends were socially active in positive ways, such as participating in sports at school or completing their homework on time,"[25] writes Valerie Ulene, a board-certified specialist in preventive medicine in Los Angeles.

Teen decision making is not entirely guided by peer pressure, however. During this time in their lives, adolescents and teenagers are trying to define themselves as individuals. They are trying to establish an identity that is separate from that of their parents. As part of this process, many teens follow the lead of their friends, taking cues from their ideas and actions. "They tend to mimic their peers' behaviors and adopt the same attitudes," Ulene writes. "Conforming to social norms helps them redefine themselves while earning them acceptance and approval. Fitting in simply feels good."[26]

These are the same types of influences at play when teens make the choice to engage in bullying. Teens who see their peers bullying others may come to think of this behavior as normal and acceptable. A study released in 2012 validates the importance of peer behavior in teen decision making. Researchers Sameer Hinduja of Florida Atlantic University and Justin W.

Patchin of the University of Wisconsin, Eau Claire, sought to understand the extent to which adolescents influenced each other in the context of cyberbullying. Hinduja and Patchin analyzed data from a random sample of forty-four hundred sixth-through twelfth-grade students from thirty-three schools in the southern United States.

As far as peer influence, Hinduja and Patchin found that those students who reported having many friends who participated in some form of cyberbullying at school were far more likely to engage in it themselves. Only 4 percent of the responders whose friends did not cyberbully at school admitted to doing it themselves, and 63 percent who said "all" or "most" of their friends cyberbullied classmates in the past thirty days admitted that they had done the same.

Bullies and Their Parents

Even before children start school and begin interacting with peers, they get many of their ideas on how to treat others from their parents. Most of the time these ideas are not taught in a conventional way. Instead, they are internalized by young people who observe how their parents treat them and others as well as how parents interact with one another.

Jim Mason, now fifty-two, learned at an early age that bullying could be an acceptable means to get his own way. His father had an abrasive manner and frequently used a loud voice when dealing with other people. "It didn't seem to matter if it was a guy refereeing my PeeWee hockey match or a teacher he thought was being unfair to one of us kids, or a waiter who was slow to bring our food," says Mason. "Being a bully was just his normal, fallback position. For us kids, that was just what fathers did."[27]

Looking back on those days, Mason says he is embarrassed that he adopted his father's ways—being sarcastic or

"Being a bully was just his normal, fallback position. For us kids, that was just what fathers did."[27]

—Jim Mason, age fifty-two, recalling being bullied by his father.

Young people often model behaviors after their parents. Being physically or emotionally abused by a parent or seeing one parent treat his or her spouse in those ways can lead a child to believe that bullying behaviors are acceptable and even advantageous.

sharp-tongued with his friends and later with his own family. An incident at work finally made him realize that he too had become a bully. He eventually sought counseling, and that made him rethink his bullying ways. Mason says that although he is no longer a bully, he thinks back on the things he has said with shame:

> I think about the words I used to use to my own family— I wish I'd known then how terrible that made them feel. I know it, because I used to feel like that when my dad would get going on us when I was young. That's the terrible part, you can't un-say things. I know my wife and kids love me, but I'd give everything to be able to take back some of those awful things I said.[28]

A Family Dynamic That Can Lead to Bullying

Like Mason, young people who bully their peers are likely to have witnessed or experienced similar behavior within their own families. This was the finding of University of Cincinnati sociologist Elizabeth Sweeney. Sweeney reviewed research from England, Germany, Norway, Japan, South Africa, and the United States in examining the phenomenon of bullying in young people between the ages of nine and sixteen. She found that youth who experience bullying at home come to see such behavior as a normal way to interact with others. Sweeney writes,

> Children who experience hostility, abuse, physical discipline and other aggressive behaviors by their parents are more likely to model that behavior in their peer relationships. Children learn from their parents how to behave and interact with others. So if they're learning about aggression and angry words at home, they will tend to use these behaviors as coping mechanisms when they interact with their peers.[29]

Some experts have researched the types of families in which bullies grow up. North Dakota State University professor Laura DeHaan explains that somewhat of a pattern of parent-child interaction has emerged from their study:

> Bullies tend to come from families that are characterized as having little warmth or affection. These families also report trouble sharing their feelings and usually rate themselves as feeling less close to each other. Parents of bullies also tend to use inconsistent discipline and little monitoring of where their children are throughout the day. Sometimes parents of bullies have very punitive and rigid discipline styles, with physical punishment being very common. Bullies also report less feelings of closeness to their siblings.[30]

Two Views of Cool

Psychologists know that peer approval can make bullying seem acceptable. It can also serve as a reward. New research indicates that age can also influence how bullies are perceived.

In 2012 Jaana Juvonen, a psychology professor at the University of California, Los Angeles, led a study of bullying in schools. For the study, researchers interviewed more than two thousand sixth-graders from ethnically diverse public middle schools in the Los Angeles area. Juvonen and her team were surprised to find that middle school bullies were considered some of the coolest kids in school. Juvonen then expanded the interviews to fourth- and fifth-graders. The team found that these younger students did not see bullies as cool. Instead, bullies in this age group were disliked and avoided. "Clearly, there's something about the school environment that makes bullies more valued among their peers in sixth grade," says Juvonen. "Think about all the changes that kids go through when they transfer from elementary school to middle school. The school not only becomes an average seven times larger than their elementary school, but now they go from one [class] period to the next, having a different teacher in each and also different classmates."

Because it can be scary and confusing, Juvonen explains, the situation "probably calls forth a primal tendency to rely on dominance behaviors." The bullies—stronger and more self-assured, are seen as being in charge, and that gives them power and status—as well as a boost to their egos.

Quoted in Judy Lin, "Psychologist's Studies Makes Sense of Bullying," UCLA Newsroom, May 3, 2012. http://news room.ucla.edu.

The Bully-Victim

Friends and family are not the only ones who influence bullying behavior. Researcher Olweus found that about 15 percent of bullies had experienced the other end of bullying: they had been bullied. Olweus termed this group of bullies *bully-victims* to differentiate them from what he called *pure bullies*. Bully-victims, he found, are lower functioning than many of their peers and often suffer from learning disabilities such as attention deficit disorder (ADD). They are bullied as often—or even more often—than they bully others. Not surprisingly, bully-victims lack the social confidence and bravado of bullies who have never been treated this way.

Scott, a fifteen-year-old from Canada, was interviewed by researcher Deborah Ellis. He admits that he has bullied others most of his life—and has been bullied himself just as long. "It's been like the survival of the fittest," he says. "You get picked on, you see other people being picked on, and you start picking on people, too. . . . You don't really want to be the target. It takes some pressure off you if you put it onto somebody else."[31]

Kyle, who was bullied relentlessly by classmates throughout elementary and middle school, says that he was both relieved and flattered when the boys who bullied him began asking him to join them in their aggression toward other students. He found it turned the frustration from being bullied by his peers onto younger students:

> I was always getting teased because of my weight. It wasn't funny teasing—it was really mean, like calling me names. But I ended up bullying kids younger than me. I made fun of their clothes, their shoes, the way they talked. I'd pick on kids who weren't good readers or dumber in math than me. I'd sometimes hit them too. And the guys that picked on me went easier on me.[32]

The Influence of an Audience

Scott, the Canadian teen interviewed by Ellis, learned that having an appreciative audience of his peers while bullying was a strong motivator. Scott remembers that during elementary school he targeted a boy named Jim, who was from a very poor family. "Everyone went after him—the whole school," Scott says. "He smelled. His family was dirt poor. His parents delivered the free shopping news around town, so you know they didn't have anything."[33]

Scott recalls the positive reaction of his friends when, one day at lunch, he dumped an open fruit cup into the boy's backpack. Though he now realizes it was a hurtful episode for Jim, at the time Scott considered the stunt a success. It made him look especially brave in front of some of his classmates—a feeling he had not experienced before:

At the time, it felt like a victory. I even felt brave, coming up with the idea, sneaking over to his bag—heart pumping in case a teacher came by—dumping the fruit cup in and running away. Like I'd just performed a dangerous, important mission. All my friends were like, "Way to go!" and laughing about the mess in the bag.[34]

Influences Specifically Related to Cyberbullying

Although boys make up the majority of physical and verbal bullies, girls are estimated to make up slightly more than half of those who are involved in cyberbullying. Psychologists say that there are likely a number of reasons for that. One reason is the society in which they are raised. For generations, many girls and women have been raised to be less aggressive and more passive in certain situations. As a result, they tend to be less confrontational in face-to-face interactions. Being able to bully without physical confrontation is more comfortable for many cyberbullies.

Another reason why many girls and young women take part in cyberbullying is that because it is done using electronic

From an early age, many girls are taught to be less confrontational than their male peers. Because of this, teen girls and young women often prefer to bully others by spreading rumors or by tormenting their victims online, where the computer screen provides a barrier to personal contact.

devices, they do not have to witness the humiliation or pain caused by such bullying. According to a study published in a 2012 article in the *International Journal of Cyber Criminology*, "Females can talk about another female behind her back or harass her online without ever having to look in her face to see her reaction. It is easy to react more brazenly without having to face the effect of your behavior."[35]

Regardless of whether it is a girl or a boy who is doing the cyberbullying, one aspect of online bullying can be particularly influential: the presence of online bystanders. Just as an audience of bystanders can spur on a physical or verbal bully, the presence of bystanders on social media sites can influence the cyberbully. They can do so by commenting favorably on the cyberbully's posts or by forwarding hurtful posts to more people, thus continuing the cycle of bullying and the misery that accompanies it.

The damage increases for the victim of cyberbullying and frequently can become overwhelming. As one fourteen-year-old cyberbullying victim from New York posted on a website for the Cyberbullying Research Center, "It makes me feel bad and rather depressed. Like I don't want to be part of this world anymore."[36]

Clues from the Bully's Brain

Besides the influences of peers and parents that can sometimes make bullying seem an acceptable behavior, there is another strong influence over which a teen has absolutely no control. That is the development of the brain. Although some people continue to be bullies well into adulthood, many people

Mental Disorders and Bullying

Experts have identified a new factor that may be influential in bullying behavior: mental disorders. A study released in 2012 by researchers at Brown University analyzed responses from parents of approximately sixty-four thousand children between the ages of six and seventeen who had been identified as bullies and who also had been found to have a mental health disorder.

Young people identified as bullies were more than twice as likely as other young people to suffer from anxiety, depression, and ADD. Youth identified as bullies in the study were six times more likely to be diagnosed with oppositional defiant disorder, which is characterized by episodes of hostility and anger toward parents, teachers, and other adults.

Such findings are not surprising to psychologists like Alan Hilfer of Brooklyn's Maimonides Medical Center. According to Hilfer, such disorders "often lead to impulsive and at times aggressive behaviors" that are common among bullies. Adds Hilfer, "They can be depressed, fearful, and they often take out some of their anger and frustration on others down the pecking order."

Quoted in Lara Salahi, "Bullies Nearly Twice as Likely to Have Mental Health Disorder," ABC News, October 22, 2012. http://abcnews.go.com.

grow out of such behavior as they mature. What scientists are learning is that how and when brains develop during the teen years might actually play a part in bullying behavior.

For many years scientists assumed that the brain was completely grown by the time a child turns ten. However, from experiments and studies done by the National Institutes of Health (NIH), scientists have learned that until about age twenty-five, a young person's brain is virtually unfinished. One important advance in the twentieth century that made such research possible was the introduction of highly sensitive instruments that allow doctors to see different areas of a living person's brain in far greater detail than ever before. One of the most valuable of these instruments is the magnetic resonance imaging (MRI) machine, that can—among other things—provide images of how the brain develops and what parts of the brain are active in a range of different situations.

Using MRIs, the NIH carried out a large number of brain scans to study more than one hundred young people throughout the stages of their growth. The project found that human brains go through very radical changes between ages twelve and twenty-five. Until then, although the brain is 90 percent grown, it remains basically unfinished—and that can make all the difference why bullying, reckless driving, and other impulsive behaviors are far more common during this stage of life.

The Unfinished Brain

While the brain itself does not actually grow very much between the ages of twelve and twenty-five, it goes through a massive reorganization during this time—a transformation that science journalist David Dobbs compares to "a network and wiring upgrade."[37] This upgrade occurs in several places in the brain, one of which is the corpus callosum, which is the area between the brain's right and left hemispheres.

Until that happens, the brain's frontal lobes are not fully connected, and that explains the big difference in how teens make decisions. "It's the part of the brain that says: 'Is this a good idea? What is the consequence of this action?'" notes pediatric neurologist Frances Jensen. "It's not that [those between twelve and twenty-five] don't have a frontal lobe. And they can use it. But they're going to access it more slowly."[38]

The reason for the frontal lobe being so sluggish is that it lacks myelin, a fatty white coating that insulates the axons, which are the long nerve fibers of the brain. Myelin production in the brain is usually not complete until adulthood, which means that during adolescence the axons are not coated with myelin and signals do not get transmitted freely. As a result, the two halves of the brain cannot communicate accurately. However, as myelin production in the brain increases, communication between the axons increases up to one hundred times faster. That development makes it more likely that the individual will be able to weigh the consequences of a particular action, such as bullying, beforehand.

> "It's not that [those between twelve and twenty-five] don't have a frontal lobe. And they can use it. But they're going to access it more slowly."[38]
>
> —Frances Jensen, a pediatric neurologist.

Finding Pleasure in Pain

One of the key aspects of bullying is causing another person physical or emotional pain, and that seems to be one of the rewards a bully finds pleasurable. Scientists have long wondered why bullies who are successful in causing such pain find it rewarding.

Though the lack of important connections in the unfinished brain affects all teenagers, the brains of certain teens are teaching researchers a great deal about a bully's reaction to other people's pain. Researchers at the University of Chicago have used brain-scan technology to study whether a bully's brain may respond to violence in a different way than the brain of a person who is not a bully. What they have learned is that some bullies actually enjoy the pain—both physical and emotional—of other people and are

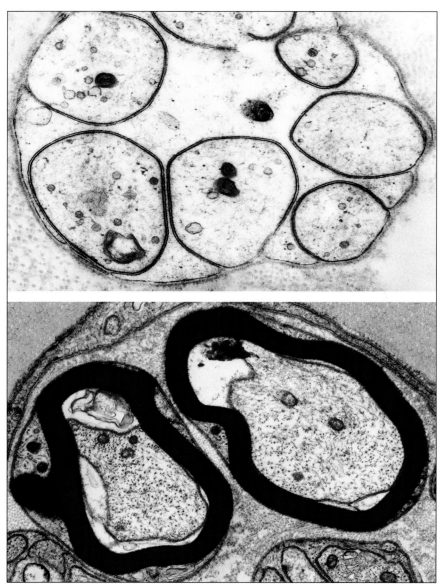

An electron micrograph shows the difference between a nerve fiber lacking myelin (top) and one that has this protective coating (bottom). The nerve fibers in teens and young adults are still developing this coating, which helps the halves of the brain communicate and recognize the consequences of actions.

thereby rewarded when a victim suffers pain or humiliation.

The scientists studied a group of eight sixteen- to eighteen-year-old boys who had been diagnosed with aggressive conduct disorder because of their histories of behaviors such as bullying, committing vandalism, using or threatening someone with a weapon, and stealing. In their research, the scientists compared those boys to another group of boys in the same age range who had no previous history of bullying or other aggressive behaviors.

The two groups of boys were shown video clips of painful situations—some accidental, others intentional. For example, one video showed a heavy mixing bowl accidentally falling on someone's hands, whereas another showed a person closing a piano lid on a player's fingers or someone purposely stepping on another person's foot. While they were watching the video clips, the boys were wired to an MRI machine that would show how different parts of their brains reacted to what they were watching.

Surprising Results

The researchers were confident that they would see a difference in the way the brains of the boys in the two groups reacted to the videos. They predicted that the bullies' brains would show very little evidence of empathy, a common human sympathetic response to seeing other people in pain. Instead, they expected to see a type of emotional coldness or indifference. However, when they saw how profound the difference was between the two groups, they were amazed.

For example, rather than showing indifference while seeing others in pain, the bullies showed a much more active response. Their brains were far more active than the group of nonbullies, but not in the empathy parts of the brain. Instead, it was in the brain's amygdala and ventral striatum that the response occurred—two parts of the brain that typically become active when a person experiences something pleasurable. "We think it means that they [the bullies] like seeing people in pain," says psychologist Benjamin Lahey, the coauthor of the study. "If that is true, they are getting positively reinforced every time they bully and are aggressive to other people."[39]

Besides showing the bullies' pleasure upon seeing people in pain, the MRI brain scans revealed another fascinating aspect of the brains of bullies: the scans showed that the part of the brain that helps regulate emotions is inactive in many of the bullies they studied. That means, for example, that if someone accidentally bumped into a bully in the school cafeteria line, the bully would likely have difficulty keeping his temper in check, making it probable that he would react by lashing out at the person who bumped him.

Lahey and other researchers say that such discoveries might someday open avenues for reducing bullying. For now, though, the data gleaned from such new studies is invaluable in explaining the many influences that can cause a teen to engage in bullying behavior.

Chapter Three

The Consequences of Bullying

Teens often fail to think about the consequences of their actions. Many do not contemplate what *might* happen if they text while driving, or what *might* result from sharing test answers with another student, or what *might* be the outcome of posting nasty comments about another kid on a social media page. If they actually thought about the possible consequences of their actions—even momentarily—it is likely that they would make very different choices.

Hurt and Overweight

One of those hurtful choices was made by several classmates of Margie Ellison. From the time she was in fourth grade until she was in eighth grade, Ellison was bullied almost every day at school. "I was overweight back then," she says.

> And in my school, that was the number-one reason kids got teased. They called me "Large Marge," which really hurt my feelings, and even talking about it today—the whole experience comes flooding back. It makes me feel like cringing just talking about being called names like that. The girls in my class would whisper comments about the size of my clothes, and the boys would pick up the teasing and join right in. And I'd try to act like I didn't care, so I wouldn't give them the satisfaction of seeing me cry.[40]

Now a college student, Ellison says that the bullying affected her life in a number of painful ways. She tried dozens of diets but without lasting success. The more she was bullied, the more depressed she felt, so the more she turned to food for comfort. "I'd come home from school, stressed and miserable, and the only thing that seemed to make me feel better was eating," she admits. "I'd go right for the cookies and soda."[41]

By eighth grade she was so desperate to lose weight that she became bulimic, making herself vomit after eating so she would not gain weight. Her frequent vomiting eventually caused an irregular heartbeat. "That was my wake-up call," Margie says:

I finally got into counseling, which really helped. I learned how to manage my weight in a healthy way and to stop listening to the bullying. It had become so bad that I was bullying myself—every time I looked in the mirror I was imagining what the bullies would say—it was horrible! I had actually become my own bully, my counselor told me. It took a while, but the counseling helped a lot. I'm not stressing anymore, and I'm eating healthy. I've got some good friends, too, who would never think of saying mean things about another person's appearance.[42]

A Wide Range of Effects

Anyone who is bullied—especially children and teens—can suffer a wide range of negative effects. Victims of bullying frequently suffer from higher levels of stress and anxiety because they do not know when the next bullying episode will occur. Being bullied by fellow students also impacts schoolwork and grades. Survey results published in the *Journal of Early Adolescence* show that "a high level of bullying by schoolmates is consistently related to academic disengagement and poor

Studies reveal that students who are severely bullied experience a drop in academic performance. A preoccupation with the bullying can lead victims to disengage from their schoolwork and fall behind in their studies.

grades."[43] That survey involved thirty-six hundred students in the United Kingdom who were interviewed about their experiences with bullying. Researchers found that 56 percent of high school students who said they had been the target of bullying believed that it was having an effect on their education. Those students reported they were more likely to get a D or lower on a report card while dealing with the stresses of being bullied.

Rob, now a junior in high school, is not surprised by this. He endured a great deal of bullying when he was in middle school because he had a severe stutter. He was a good student, especially in social studies and English, but his speech impediment made him an easy target for bullies:

> When I got called on, I'd get nervous sometimes, and I could just feel I was going to start [stuttering]. Besides having a hard time getting the words out, I tended to

blink a lot when I stuttered too. And there were these three guys in my class who would start stuttering too—just to make fun of me. And they'd do this weird blinking too, which made me feel so embarrassed. I would be like, "Oh my gosh, is that how I look to everybody?" I started getting so nervous whenever I got called on that I would start stuttering worse than ever.[44]

Rob says that he tried to cope with the bullying but knows now that that he went about it in the wrong way. Though he was a good student and liked school, he decided to stop raising his hand when he knew an answer. And if a teacher called on him, he would purposely pretend not to know an answer, just so the bullies would not make fun of his stutter:

Instead of answering when the teacher called on me, I just said I didn't know the answer. Or sometimes I didn't talk at all and just shrugged. It was so frustrating at first to pretend to not know anything, when I usually did—especially in Mr. Larson's American history class, which was my favorite class. But at least I didn't get mocked as much. But I wish now that I hadn't pretended that way because I think Mr. Larson was kind of disappointed in me, and he was one of the best teachers I ever had. Someday I think I'm going to go back and tell him why I stopped raising my hand in his class.[45]

Pulling Away from People

One of the most damaging results of bullying is that victims tend to become isolated from others. The embarrassment of being bullied in front of classmates or humiliated by vicious texts or posts makes it difficult to carry on as though nothing were happening. The response is often to pull away from interactions with other people, even people who were considered friends. "It's way more embarrassing if the person hassling you does it in front of your friends," says one ninth-grader who has been a victim of bullying. "I'd rather just keep a low profile and be on my own. And sometimes I think my friends aren't real comfortable either, like maybe the [bully] is going to start going after them. I've seen it happen to other guys, and it really can turn into an ugly situation."[46]

Being cyberbullied frequently results in the isolation of the victim, who feels that he or she has been publicly shamed. Fourteen-year-old Heather isolated herself after a former friend posted on her Facebook page a very unflattering photograph taken at a sleepover party. In the photo Heather was posing with a beer bottle in her hand, pretending to drink. Heather says when that picture was posted, it was seen by everyone she knew, and a lot of people she didn't know. The mean comments that continued for weeks afterwards online caused her great embarrassment:

> I cried when I found out what she did. I didn't know if I was more devastated that my friend would do something like that or just that the picture was so hideous. But everyone I knew saw it. I absolutely didn't want to go to school the next day. I kept thinking about how people at school would laugh at me or say sarcastic stuff like "Great photo!" or "Wow, never knew you had a drinking problem!" That was all I could think about, being embarrassed in front of everybody, and having no one to defend me.[47]

Heather says that when she returned to school, she purposely distanced herself from people with whom she usually felt comfortable. She ate her lunch in an empty classroom or even in the bathroom. She did not linger at her locker to talk with classmates as she usually did. She even lied to her volleyball coach, faking an injury so she could skip practice and thus avoid any interaction with her teammates.

"I hated the whole situation," she says. "I missed three big games that I really could have played in. I missed sitting on the bench with my teammates—I couldn't even do that since I had missed a bunch of practices. And I still felt like everybody was talking about the stupid photo online. That ranks as the worst of my memories of that school year."[48]

Panic and Depression

Besides becoming isolated from friends and classmates, victims of bullying often suffer from a range of emotional problems. "We see kids coming in with issues ranging from insomnia and anger to depression and anxiety," says counselor Anna Mann. "They often have difficulty connecting with other kids because

Lower Test Scores

Academics suffer when kids are bullied, in part because those who are targeted by bullies tend to stay home from school a lot. Researchers have found a correlation between a high rate of school absenteeism and low scores on standardized tests. Researchers at the University of Virginia reported these findings after surveying more than seventy-three hundred ninth-graders about their experiences with bullying. The survey, led by Dewey Cornell, a clinical psychologist and professor of education, found that the passing grades on those standardized tests were between 3 percent and 6 percent lower in schools in which severe bullying had been reported. "This study supports the case for school-wide bullying-prevention programs as a step to improve school climate and facilitate academic potential," says Cornell. "Our society does not permit harassment and abuse of adults in the workplace, and the same protections should be afforded to children in school."

Quoted in American Psychological Association, "Bullying May Contribute to Lower Test Scores," August 7, 2011. www.apa.org.

they are embarrassed and ashamed because they feel they've been humiliated and their peers are all aware of it."[49]

Ray, a twenty-two-year-old automobile mechanic living in Milwaukee, Wisconsin, says he experienced such symptoms at age fifteen when he came out as gay. While he braced himself for negative reactions from some of his classmates and friends, he says the bullying he endured turned out to be far more stressful than he had ever imagined:

> First I told my parents, and that actually wasn't nearly as bad as I thought it would be. But kids at school, that was different. Some tried to be cool with it, but they really weren't. Some of them were pretty hostile. They were more worried that other kids would think they were gay too because they sometimes hung out with me. So it was a nightmare for a pretty long time. [There was] a lot of drama, name-calling, getting shoved in the halls, the whistling at me—that didn't stop for a long time.[50]

As a result of the constant abuse, Ray says he began having panic attacks during which he would experience a pounding heartbeat, flushed face, dizziness, and difficulty breathing. As the weeks and months went by, he became depressed and had thought about hurting himself to escape his pain. "I felt worthless—that's the only way to describe it," he says.

> The worst part was that I didn't know how to confront the people who were mocking me, and there weren't many people in my corner. I felt kind of like I was on my own island, and really mixed up. It was the worst at night, when I was trying to fall asleep. I just couldn't get the [bullies'] voices out of my head. It was kind of like a loop with the word *faggot* going over and over in my brain. I felt like I was going insane.[51]

Bullying and Suicide

The most dangerous consequence of bullying is when victims start to think the only way out of their situation is suicide. In fact, there is now a term for suicide committed by a person as a result of being incessantly bullied: *bullycide*. A Yale University study found that victims of bullying are five times more likely than nonvictims to consider suicide. A separate study done in Great Britain found that among ten- to fourteen-year-olds, 44 percent of suicides are linked to bullying.

Kenneth Weishuhn is one tragic example of bullycide. A fourteen-year-old freshman at South O'Brien High School in Paulina, Iowa, Weishuhn had come out as gay to family and friends in the spring of 2012. As the news spread, Weishuhn was subjected to a torrent of bullying, both face to face and online. Not long afterward he hanged himself in the family's garage.

His sister Kayla says that many of his tormentors had been her brother's friends, and that was particularly devastating. He got violent threats on his cellphone. At one point some of his former friends even started a Facebook page dedicated to posting hateful messages about him and other gay people. "People who were originally his friends, they kind of turned on him," Kayla told one reporter. "A lot of people, they either joined in or they were too scared to say anything."[52]

Some well-known advocates for teens going through the difficult process of coming out lent their voices to the outrage over what happened to Weishuhn. Singer Madonna, an outspoken champion of young people who are brave enough to be honest about their sexuality, was one of these. Soon after Weishuhn's death, during her European tour, Madonna used a large photograph of him and photos of six other gay young people who had killed themselves as a backdrop for her song "Nobody Knows Me." She dedicated the song to these teens.

> **"I just couldn't get the [bullies'] voices out of my head. It was kind of like a loop with the word *faggot* going over and over in my brain."[51]**
>
> —*Ray, twenty-two, a mechanic from Wisconsin.*

Veteran pop singer Madonna is an outspoken champion of young people who are brave enough to be open about their sexuality. Soon after the death of Kenneth Weishuhn in 2012, she dedicated a song in her concert tour to Weisuhn and other young gay people who had killed themselves after being bullied.

Many schools throughout Iowa held candlelight vigils in Weishuhn's memory. Many experts say that Weishuhn's death should be a wake-up call for parents, teachers, and students about the dangers gay youth face from bullies in their schools and communities. Calla Rongerude, the executive director of

One Iowa, a lesbian, gay, bisexual, and transgender (LGBT) advocacy group, praised Weishuhn for the courage he showed in coming out. She also reminded young people that bullying is never appropriate: "Kenneth made the brave choice to live his life openly and fully, and he was targeted at school with taunts, hurtful online organizing against him, and even death threats. No one, especially the most vulnerable members of our community, should face bullying and threats of violence simply for being who they are."[53]

The Effects on the Brain

The trauma of bullying can go beyond emotional distress. Experts say that bullying sometimes brings about physical changes in the brain. Scientists have long understood that the human brain continues to grow and change for years after birth. A person's experiences during childhood and adolescence help to shape brain development and wiring. Scientists have learned, too, that certain traumatic events, such as sexual or physical abuse in childhood or adolescence, can damage parts of the brain. This damage is known as scarring, and it can last a lifetime.

Psychiatrist Martin Teicher and a team of researchers at Harvard Medical School studied the brains of young adults between the ages of eighteen and twenty-five. The study subjects, none of whom had ever been exposed to domestic violence or sexual abuse, were asked about their experiences with bullying. Those who had been targeted by bullies at a younger age were given brain scans. The results, published in the *American Journal of Psychiatry*, showed that the brains of those who had been bullied had significantly underdeveloped connections in the corpus callosum, the part of the brain that helps the right and left hemispheres communicate.

Such damage has predictable results, experts say. When the corpus callosum is not completely developed, important decision-making functions do not work as well, and messages between the right and left hemisphere of the brain do not get transmitted either as quickly or as accurately as they should. In the twenty-first century, with newer, more precise and more sensitive instruments that can scan a brain in great detail, researchers are able to visualize how certain parts of the brain are affected by bullying.

The Importance of Who and When

In subsequent research, Teicher and his colleagues found that who is doing the bullying and the victim's age at the time of the events can make a difference in how the brain responds. They found that verbal bullying by one's parents or peers causes more severe damage in the brain. In one of Teicher's studies, the researchers looked at adults between eighteen and twenty-five who had no history of physical or sexual abuse as children. They were asked to rate their exposure to parent and peer verbal abuse when they were children.

After their interviews, each of the subjects was given a brain scan. The results revealed that each person who reported experiencing verbal abuse from their peers or parents during middle school years had an underdeveloped corpus callosum. The psychological tests given to all subjects in the study showed that this same group of individuals had higher levels of anxiety, depression, hostility, and drug abuse than others in the study.

Verbal abuse that occurs during the middle school years is especially damaging, the study found, because it is during this period that brain connections are rapidly developing. Young people who experience bullying at this age are more likely to self-repeat, which means their brains will adopt the nasty comments made about them as truth. Teicher explains the seriousness of this phenomenon:

> When you're told things about yourself—when you're told that you're fat or that you're ugly or that you're a spaz—you wind up in a situation where that voice gets incorporated in your thinking. You wind up in a repetitive pattern of humiliation. We're wounded in a way that's enduring by our exposure. It's really important to be mindful—and very important, I think, for teachers in school to not allow it.[54]

The middle school years are a particularly vulnerable time for adolescents. Studies reveal that because the brains of middle school teens are still developing, negative comments can become ingrained as truth in these young people and influence their self-image throughout their lives.

Many brain experts worry about what they see as a growing trend of incivility in schools—where bullying seems to be on the rise. This trend alarms R. Douglas Fields, a neuroscience expert at the National Institute of Child Health and Human Development. Fields warns that schools could become "an incubator for developing brains with abnormalities . . . and an elevated risk of psychiatric problems."[55]

The Long-Term Effects of Bullying

Bullying results in other long-term damage that may be just as worrisome. Psychologists say that many of the most troubling problems surface months and even years after the bullying stops, and they may last a lifetime. In a study by Warwick University in England and Duke University in North Carolina, psychologists tracked fourteen hundred people between the ages of nine and twenty-six.

They found that participants in the study who had been involved in bullying—either as a bully or a victim—experienced outcomes that tended to be worse than the average for people who had not been exposed to bullying. For example, victims of bullies were likely to experience more serious illnesses, more poverty, and more mental health problems. And those who had been bullies were more likely to have been fired from a job or to be in a violent relationship.

A Bully's Regret

In her book *Sticks and Stones: Defeating the Culture of Bullying and Rediscovering the Power of Character and Empathy*, Emily Bazelon reports that bullies and their victims often have unresolved issues years later. She introduces readers to Adam, a tenth-grader who was constantly bullied by a boy named Brad. When Adam was in his thirties, he found Brad on Facebook and decided to contact him and see what he remembered about their history. The following is an excerpt from Brad's reply:

> Even now, years later, I can't understand what was going through our minds or even why we felt the need to do this. . . . I knew it was wrong, but that didn't seem to matter at the time. I remember going up to you and apologizing, in part because I knew I would be getting suspended, but also because I was really affected by the way everyone was reacting. It was only in this context that it really hit me. I had positioned myself as something of a ringleader and gave up a substantial part of "me" in the process. I began to realize later in high school how wrong I was, and I still think about it to this day.

Quoted in Emily Bazelon, *Sticks and Stones: Defeating the Culture of Bullying and Rediscovering the Power of Character and Empathy.* New York: Random House, 2013, p. 6.

Interestingly, however, those with the most severe long-lasting effects were those who had been bullied as children and then had become bullies themselves. This is the group that researcher Olweus had labeled *bully-victims* years before. The bully-victims were far more likely than others to commit crimes, drink to excess, or take illegal drugs as they reached adulthood. They were at greater risk than others for developing health problems as adults and were six times more likely to be diagnosed with a serious illness. They were also more likely to become heavy smokers and to develop a psychiatric disorder.

Dieter Wolke, one of the study's leaders, says such data should serve as a wake-up call to address bullying as a serious problem with lifelong consequences. "We cannot continue to dismiss bullying as a harmless, almost inevitable, part of growing up," he warns. "We need to change this mindset and acknowledge this as a serious problem."[56] The biggest obstacle to making this happen might be teens themselves. Making sure they understand the consequences is the responsibility of the adults around them; making good choices, however, is up to them.

Chapter Four

Ways to Stop the Bullying

Given the potentially dangerous consequences of bullying, it is not surprising that people have been searching for effective ways to discourage young people from engaging in such behavior. For example, most school districts in the United States have had policies against bullying for years. Students who were caught harassing other classmates were punished by means of a detention or a suspension. "It was pretty simple years ago," says Marlene Lutz, a retired high school math teacher.

> You sat the kid down, made him or her apologize to whoever got bullied, and if that didn't seem adequate, you called the parents. If it happened again, they'd get a suspension for a day or two. Usually that worked; the kids ended up settling it. But it's so different these days—an awful lot of the bullying seems to take place outside of school or online. . . . So it's far more difficult to address bullying today.[57]

Presidential Support

The US president and first lady, who are parents of two teenage girls, have joined the public dialogue on the topic of bullying. In March 2011 President Barack Obama and First Lady Michelle Obama hosted the first-ever White House Conference on Bullying Prevention. Teachers, students, policy makers, and families of bullied young people who had committed suicide gathered to discuss ideas on how to stop bullying in schools. Speaking at the conference, President Obama said, "If there's one goal of this conference, it's to dispel the myth that bullying is just a harmless rite of passage or an inevitable part of growing up. It's not."[58]

In addition to the White House Conference on Bullying Prevention, the Obama administration has also voiced support for the Safe School Improvement Act. The act aims to solve the problem of bullying experienced by LGBT students, who are frequently the victims of harassment. "I don't know what it's like to be picked on for being gay," the president said in a video

In 2011, President Barack Obama addresses a White House conference on bullying. Educators and policy makers gathered at this meeting to make the problem more visible and to discuss ways to take action against bullying behaviors in schools.

posted on the White House website and on YouTube. "But I do know what it's like to grow up feeling that sometimes you don't belong. It's tough."[59]

Bullying and the Law

Other people around the country have come to agree that bullying is a force that is impacting young people in highly negative ways. Lawmakers are using the tools at their disposal to help fight bullying. As of 2014 all US states except Montana had passed some type of antibullying law.

The laws vary widely from state to state, and they vary in scope, the amount of protection afforded to students, and even have different definitions of bullying. For example, 40 states have laws requiring schools to add some form of anti-bullying education to their curriculum. This might include social-emotional learning exercises that teach students how to prevent bullying or ways that bystanders can become involved in curtailing bullying behavior. However, states including Arizona, Missouri, Kentucky, and six others have no such laws. Another type of law, such as one in Minnesota, addresses the bullying of students based on sexual orientation or gender identity. And some new laws—passed in twelve states—include criminal sanctions for bullies. These include suspension or expulsion from school or, in severe cases, time in jail.

> "I . . . know what it's like to grow up feeling that sometimes you don't belong. It's tough."[59]
>
> —President Barack Obama.

Bullies and Jail?

The notion of bullies serving jail time in extreme circumstances is not unprecedented. In one highly publicized incident in 2010, Tyler Clementi, an eighteen-year-old freshman at Rutgers University, committed suicide after his roommate, Dharun Ravi, set up a webcam in their room. Ravi used the webcam to spy on Clementi having a sexual encounter with another male student. Ravi then shared the video with his friends. Calling Ravi's actions a hate crime, the judge sentenced Ravi to serve twenty days in jail.

And although some believe that in such cases bullies should be prosecuted, others are uncomfortable with the idea of jail time for bullying. But Liza, a longtime victim of bullying because of a speech impediment, disagrees:

> When you purposely wound someone's self-esteem by bullying them, it can be more damaging than attacking them with your fists—and people can be sentenced to jail for doing that. When you step back and see the result—grieving moms and dads of young people who've taken their own lives or kids who are using [drugs or alcohol], self-medicating because of the depression and anxiety they experience when they endure bullying—you realize just how destructive it can be to a person's life.[60]

Using a Cyberbully's Tools
for a Good Cause

One family, distraught over the damage done by cyberbullies, has decided to use the same online tools employed by bullies to show other teens the immense hurt they cause. This effort, the family hopes, will get young people to think about their actions before taking part in mean-spirited social media posts and cellphone texts. The event that brought this about took place in August 2014 in Bay Village, Ohio. It involved a group of high school students who thought it would be funny to get a fifteen-year-old boy with autism to take an ugly variation of an ice bucket challenge, record it, and then post it on social media.

Ice bucket challenges caught on in 2014 as a way to raise money for research into a degenerative nerve disorder called amyotrophic lateral sclerosis (ALS). Hundreds of celebrities and others have taken part in this ALS fund-raiser, which works this way: Person A urges person B to take the challenge. If person B agrees, someone will dump a bucket of ice water over his or her head within twenty-four hours. But if person B does not accept the challenge, he or she must instead write a check to the ALS Society to help fund research. (In most cases, both situations lead to the person donating money to the cause.)

The group of high school students came up with a nasty variation on this idea when they goaded their victim into agreeing to take the challenge. They thought it would be hilarious, however, if instead of ice water they filled the bucket with a filthy mixture of urine, feces, spit, and cigarette butts. They forced him to strip down to his underwear and then recorded his reaction to having the disgusting sludge dumped over his head.

Thousands of people saw the video, which the bullies posted on Instagram. The victim's brother had witnessed meanness directed toward his brother before but never anything on this scale. "I mean, the first thing that popped into my mind was like, why could someone—how could someone do this?" he asked. "How could someone really be this cruel to someone?"[61]

> "The first thing that popped into my mind was like, why could someone— how could someone do this? How could someone really be this cruel to someone?"[61]
>
> —*Jacob, the brother of a fifteen-year-old autistic teen who was humiliated by bullies.*

Even though it was an excruciating video for the boy's family to watch, the family eventually decided to give their permission for the local television station to show it, hoping it would be an educational tool. The station producer said that the family hoped that seeing what happened to their son would make other families more aware of bullying. And once people could see what the bullies had done, parents might be able to have a meaningful conversation with their children about how damaging it is.

Cutting Down on Mean Posts

The social networking site Facebook has also been working to end bullying. Since the site's inception in 2004, Facebook has been very clear about its antibullying rules. Anyone who

Facebook maintains an antibullying policy that users must agree to if they wish to join the site. However, as with most social media platforms, monitoring the multitude of users and their numerous posts is difficult, leading to unchecked abuses.

uses Facebook must first agree to its policy about harassing or bullying online. "Facebook does not tolerate bullying or harassment," the company warns new users. "We allow users to speak freely on matters and people of public interest, but take action on all reports of abusive behavior directed at private individuals."[62]

With more than 1.3 billion users around the world and approximately 7.5 billion posts on Facebook weekly, policing the site for rule breakers is an impossible task—and users know it. Consequently, bullying is a common occurrence on Facebook, with an estimated 2 million complaints each week about the harassing or bullying contents of posts. In a 2011 study *Consumer Reports* estimated that 1 million of the youngest users of Facebook (those between ten and thirteen) had been bullied or threatened on the site during the previous year. Says John

Tackling Mean-Girl Bullying

One of the most damaging sorts of bullying is relationship aggression, which is also known as mean-girl bullying because it is perpetrated by girls and targets other girls. Often referred to as mean girls, these bullies gossip, spread rumors, and pointedly exclude and ignore targets to isolate and humiliate them. As a result, relationship bullying often can result in damaging and even fatal outcomes.

However, a 2014 study at the University of Missouri has developed a method of intervention that has been shown to decrease such bullying. It is called Growing Interpersonal Relationships through Learning and Systemic Supports (GIRLSS). The intervention is a ten-week process that includes group counseling for girls aged twelve to fifteen, showing them the benefits of journaling and setting goals for themselves. GIRLSS also provides training and phone support for their parents, guardians, and teachers.

Early reactions to the program have been positive; the study found a decrease in relationship bullying among the girls who took part. Notes Connie Brooks, the coauthor of the study, "Good outcomes can happen when priorities are set by schools and families to prevent and eliminate relationship aggression."

Quoted in Diamond Dixon, "Intervention Helps 'Mean Girl' Behavior, MU Researchers Find," MU News, October 1, 2014. http://munews.missouri.edu.

Venners, a social media expert, "The Internet opens a lot of doors for children to learn and grow, but it unfortunately also makes them vulnerable to bullies and online predators."[63]

Facebook has increased the number of staff whose job it is to sift through posts looking for proof of bullying or harassment. However, identifying such posts is actually not as easy as one might think. Some comments, for instance, might sound like bullying at first glance but instead might have been intended as sarcasm or irony. "Bullying is hard," says Dave Willner, a Facebook manager who investigates complaints of harassment and bullying on the site. "It's slippery to define, and it's even harder when it's writing instead of speech. Tone of voice disappears."[64]

Mathematics to the Rescue

Facebook has been working to perfect a system using complex mathematical formulas, or algorithms, to help employees scan the site's billions of posts daily and narrow the number that need to be reviewed and possibly removed from the site. This effort is being led by Henry Lieberman, a computer expert at the Massachusetts Institute of Technology. Bullied himself as a middle school student because of his weight, Lieberman was eager to find a way of identifying and flagging bullying comments within the tremendous numbers of daily Facebook posts.

Lieberman and his team developed a computer program that uses algorithms to search through enormous amounts of data. The team's algorithms search for words that are typically used by bullies, such as *fat, ugly, slut,* and *faggot.* These and other terms are part of a repository of words and phrases known as BullySpace. By pairing an algorithm with the BullySpace words, the computer flags possible bullying posts containing such words, even using the shorthand texting spellings or misspellings commonly used.

Sometimes even combinations of neutral words are used in a bullying way. Lieberman gives the example of *hamburger,* a word that is neither negative nor positive. However, when it is paired with the word *six*, for example, "I saw her eat six hamburgers," it might signal that someone is making cruel comments about someone who is overweight—a common thread in bullying posts. By checking the context, the computer could flag it for a more careful look.

> "The Internet opens a lot of doors for children to learn and grow, but it unfortunately also makes them vulnerable to bullies."[63]
>
> —*Social media expert John Venners.*

Teaching Empathy

One of the most interesting new ways Facebook is trying to eliminate bullying on its site sounds almost impossible: teaching empathy to its users. Empathy is the ability to understand the thoughts or emotions of another person—putting oneself in another person's shoes. Arthur Bejar, the director of engineering for Facebook's Protect and Care team, thinks that many of the site's users are not intending to bully others. He believes that if they knew that a particular post was causing someone distress, they would delete it.

Most of the time people rely on facial expressions and the tone of a person's voice to understand another's meaning, such as whether a comment is meant to be sarcastic. And since neither tone of voice nor facial expressions are part of a Facebook post, those posts can be easily misunderstood. Likewise, sometimes the person posting the message does not realize that his or her comments are hurtful.

> "Bullying is hard. It's slippery to define, and it's even harder when it's writing instead of speech. Tone of voice disappears."[64]
>
> —Facebook manager Dave Willner.

Bejar and his team have developed tools that Facebook members can use to provide feedback about a mean post or photograph and also to explain why they want a particular post to be removed. They are given a range of choices, including "it's embarrassing" or "it makes me feel sad." In addition, recipients are asked to explain what they think is the context of the post and how sad or embarrassed they feel. Facebook then provides them with a prewritten response that they can send to the person whose post hurt their feelings.

Bejar's team is confident that the system is having positive results. In as many as 85 percent of cases when teens receive a Facebook post that makes them feel bad, they are using one of the messages to reply to the sender. Marc Brackett, director of the Yale Center for Emotional Intelligence, is working with Facebook on the new system. He says, "When kids let someone know they've hurt their feelings in a personal way, there's a strong likelihood that the other kid will take that [post] down."[65]

A Reason to Play by the Rules

Companies like Facebook have a great deal of influence over teen behavior on their sites, which is why they are under pressure to develop rules and monitor behavior to make sure users comply with those rules. Facebook's Willner says most teens are motivated to follow the company's rules because not following them can get a user kicked off the site. Ideally, teens will use good judgment when it comes to online behavior. But it does not hurt to also know that the site is watching for bullying. "What we have over you is that your Facebook profile is of value to you," says Willner. "It's a hostage situation."[66]

Author Emily Bazelon confirms that teens place great value on their social media connections. Bazelon states, "In the course of my reporting, I'd been asking middle-school and high-school students whether they'd rather be suspended from school or from Facebook," she says, "and most of them picked school."[67]

Celebrities Speak Out

Celebrities with teen appeal carry a lot of weight by lending their voices to efforts to stop bullying. Many of those who have spoken out say they know exactly what it feels like to be bullied because they experienced bullying as teens. Fans are often surprised to learn that famous actors and musicians were once bullied. Actor Christian Bale says that for years he was beaten up regularly—kicked and punched by a group of boys. Olympic swimmer Michael Phelps says he was harassed by his classmates because he had a lisp and big ears. Singer Justin Timberlake says that he was bullied because he was not interested in sports in high school. "I grew up in Tennessee, and if you didn't play football, you were a sissy. I got slurs all the time because I was in music and art."[68]

One of the most vocal celebrities against bullying is singer and songwriter Lady Gaga, who has declared it her mission to show teens that the pain of being bullied eventually goes away. She was the victim of vicious bullying as a girl, and she says that the hurt and shame of being bullied was very painful. "I got really bullied," she remembers.

> I had a nice group of friends, but getting picked on in school—it sticks with you for life and I don't think I realized how deeply it affected me until I started to

become more successful and suddenly there's lots of pressure and you have to be a role model. I had to look inside myself and say, "Well, what do I have to offer?" Because for so many years I felt like I didn't have very much to offer.[69]

Justin Timberlake is one of many celebrities who have admitted to being bullied as teens. The popularity and influence of these willing spokespeople make it easier to spread the message of tolerance to the younger generations.

Ideas from Young People

Children and teens are also coming up with ways to encourage others to resist bullying. Christian Bucks, a second-grader at Roundtown Elementary School in York, Pennsylvania, could not help noticing a small group of classmates who always seemed to be standing off by themselves during recess. It was easy to see that they were lonely and unhappy and had no one to play with. Because they were isolated, they were easy marks for bullies.

Christian remembered a time when his father was thinking of relocating to Germany for his job. In one of the brochures for an international school, Christian read about a bench on one school playground where a lonely or shy student could sit, and classmates could identify him or her as someone who needed a friend. Christian mentioned this idea to his principal, Matthew Miller. Within a short time Roundtown Elementary School had its own new, brightly colored buddy bench.

The bench was an immediate success. Christian is hopeful that his classmates will keep an eye out for anyone sitting at the buddy bench and include him or her in conversation or games. "We show we care about others when we ask others to play," he says. "I also hope that new friendships will be made because of the buddy bench."[70]

Another novel idea was that of Caitlin Prater-Haacke, an eleventh-grader from a community north of Calgary, Alberta, in Canada. Someone broke into her locker and used Caitlin's iPad to post a tasteless Facebook status update that urged her to die. Instead of getting angry and feeling abused by unknown bullies, Caitlin decided to respond with kindness. She bought hundreds of Post-It notes and put one on every one of the school's 850 lockers early in the morning before other students arrived. On each brightly colored note she had written a positive message, such as "You're awesome" or "You're beautiful."

Many of Caitlin's classmates said that they kept the Post-Its because the notes made them feel special. "Bullying is not necessarily addressed [by schools]," Caitlin explained when a reporter asked why she had done what she did, "and people get really down about it. I wanted to do something positive—it was about due time."[71]

Bullies Outside of the Classroom

Adolescents and teens know as well as anyone that bullying can happen just about anywhere. At the middle school level, bullies often target their victims in school lunchrooms and hallways or at bus stops and on buses, away from the watchful eyes of teachers and administrators. "We can't be everywhere," says former middle school teacher Pete Reilly:

> In a perfect world, I'd have been out in the hall between classes to keep an eye on things. But it seems like so much of the time students would come up to me at my desk right after class, asking a question or making arrangements for me to help them after school. And so I didn't always see any bullying, fights, or other [problems] that happens out in the hall as the kids are changing classes.[72]

According to the National Center for Education Statistics, most bullying involving middle school students—especially sixth graders—takes place on the school bus. With 440,000 school buses transporting 24 million young people to and from school every year in the United States, it is not surprising that drivers see their share of student bullying. Some school districts hire bus monitors to keep track of such misbehavior, but many cannot afford the cost of monitors. As a result, the driver is quite often the only adult on the bus and therefore must be trained to play a key role in stopping such behavior.

Bully-Proofing the Bus

Therapist Ellen de Lara of Syracuse University believes that school districts need to deal with bullying on buses because what happens on the way to school can affect a student's en-

A Bullying App

One of the problems with reducing bullying in schools is that many students are reluctant to report it. They may feel embarrassed to have been bullied, or they may be worried that the bullying will become even worse. Even if they are bystanders rather than victims, they may still worry about being labeled a snitch. As a result, only 20 percent of students who are bullied report the incident.

In February 2015 an interesting new method of reporting bullying was launched in Florence, a city in northwest Alabama. A group of teachers had been assigned to do a project that would make an impact on their school system for their own continuing education. What they came up with was an app that would allow students to report bullying confidentially while at school. Since every student in grades five through twelve is assigned an iPad for the school year, everyone would have ready access to the app. And because the student using the app would not be seen talking to an administrator, he or she would not be identified as the one reporting the incident.

Three school campuses in Florence were selected for the pilot program. As soon as a student reports the bullying, the administrator of the school receives an e-mail, and an investigation is launched immediately. On the first day of the app's launch, one of the teachers responsible for the new app reported that two reports already had been generated.

tire day. "I want school administrators to become more aware of the problems that drivers are facing—they can't just see school bus bullying as separate from the rest of the day,"[73] she says.

Some school districts have installed cameras on their buses, and that has helped. In other cases drivers have created seating charts or have taken a photo of each child and displayed them to create a warmer, friendlier atmosphere—something that has had good results in minimizing bullying incidents. One important strategy is to teach drivers to recognize behavior indicating that a student might be particularly vulnerable.

And in cases when bullying does occur when the bus is in motion, drivers are told to pull over immediately and intervene rather than keep driving during the disturbance. "It's called the 'teachable moment,'" says bully awareness specialist Cassandra Ingham, "because it's a time when the driver can point out the problematic behavior and inform the child that what they're doing is wrong."[74]

An End to Bullying?

Whether bullying takes place on a school bus, in the classroom, or via a hateful social media post, the experience can be both traumatic and humiliating. Many teens know this. They are starting to think and talk more about this topic. As that continues, they are likely to think more as well about the choices they make.

Bullying does not have to be an inevitable part of growing up. As researcher Deborah Ellis notes, "The more we talk with each other, share our stories, and listen—particularly to those whose voices aren't often heard—the closer we move toward a just society. We can find ways to support each other, learn from each other, and create a world where we all feel welcome and respected. . . . How we choose to behave with our family, friends, and community influences the kind of world we inherit."[75]

Source Notes

Introduction: A Hurtful Choice

1. Kaitlin, interview with the author, October 13, 2014.

2. Kaitlin, interview.

3. Anna Mann, interview with the author, November 1, 2014.

Chapter One: The Faces of Bullying

4. Quoted in Emily Bazelon, *Sticks and Stones: Defeating the Culture of Bullying and Rediscovering the Power of Character and Empathy.* New York: Random House, 2013, pp. 28–29.

5. Sylvia Hall, interview with the author, October 15, 2014.

6. Quoted in Deborah Ellis, *We Want You to Know: Kids Talk About Bullying.* Regina, Saskatchewan, Canada: Coteau, 2010, p. 83.

7. Bill, interview with the author, October 13, 2014.

8. Mann, interview.

9. Gabrielle Ford with Sarah Thomson, *Gabe and Izzy: Standing Up for America's Bullied.* New York: Penguin, 2014, pp. 30–31.

10. Quoted in Ford, *Gabe and Izzy,* p. 31.

11. Amy Schultz, interview with the author, October 18, 2014.

12. Schultz, interview.

13. Quoted in Ellis, *We Want You to Know,* p. 99.

14. Quoted in Ellis, *We Want You to Know,* p. 99.

15. Quoted in Ellis, *We Want You to Know,* p. 99.

16. Quoted in Ellis, *We Want You to Know,* p. 80.

17. Quoted in Ellis, *We Want You to Know,* p. 80.

18. Jenna, interview with the author, November 7, 2014.

19. Bazelon, *Sticks and Stones,* p. 41.

20. Patty, interview with the author, October 18, 2014.

21. Quoted in Bazelon, *Sticks and Stones,* p. 11

22. Bazelon, *Sticks and Stones,* p. 12.

23. Quoted in Susan Donaldson James, "Jamey Rodemeyer Suicide: Police Open Criminal Bully Charges," ABC News, September 22, 2011. http://abcnews.go.com.

24. Quoted in Scott Stump, "Teen's Parents: After Suicide, He's Still Being Bullied," Today News, September 27, 2011. www.today.com.

Chapter Two: The Many Competing Influences on Teens

25. Valerie Ulene, "A Teen's Friends Are a Powerful Influence," *Los Angeles Times,* April 11, 2011. http://articles.latimes.com.

26. Ulene, "A Teen's Friends Are a Powerful Influence."

27. Jim Mason, interview with the author, October 30, 2014.

28. Mason, interview.

29. University of Cincinnati, "The School Bully: Does It Run in the Family?," ScienceDaily, August 5, 2008. www.science daily.com.

30. Quoted in Serge Sognonvi and Carmen Sognonvi, "Why Do Bullies Bully? The Top 5 Reasons Why People Bully Others," Urban Dojo, June 16, 2010. www.urbandojo.com.

31. Quoted in Ellis, *We Want You to Know,* p. 110.

32. Kyle, interview with the author, October 20, 2014.

33. Quoted in Ellis, *We Want You to Know*, p. 111.

34. Quoted in Ellis, *We Want You to Know,* p. 111.

35. C.D. Marcum, "Battle of the Sexes: An Examination of Male and Female Cyber Bullying," *International Journal of Cyber Criminology,* June 2012, p. 904.

36. Quoted in Sanjay Gupta, "Cyber Bully Victims 'Isolated, Dehumanized,'" *The Chart* (blog), CNN, September 21, 2010. http://thechart.blogs.cnn.com.

37. David Dobbs, "Teenage Brains," *National Geographic,* October 2011. http://ngm.nationalgeographic.com.

38. Quoted in Richard Knox, "The Teen Brain: It's Just Not Grown Up Yet," NPR, March 1, 2010. www.npr.org.

39. Quoted in John Roach, "Bullies' Brains Light Up with Pleasure as People Squirm," *National Geographic News,* November 7, 2008. http://news.nationalgeographic.com.

Chapter Three: The Consequences of Bullying

40. Margie Ellison, interview with the author, October 16, 2014.

41. Ellison, interview.

42. Ellison, interview.

43. Quoted in Tamara Christine Van Hooser, "Can Bullying Lead to Failing Grades?," GlobalPost. http://everydaylife .globalpost.com.

44. Rob, interview with the author, November 11, 2014.

45. Rob, interview.

46. Donald, interview with the author, December 2, 2014.

47. Heather, interview with the author, October 30, 2014.

48. Heather, interview.

49. Mann, interview.

50. Ray, interview with the author, October 20, 2014.

51. Ray, interview.

52. Quoted in Craig Johnson, "Wake Up Call: Gay Teen's Suicide Rocks Town," HLN, April 19, 2012. www.hlntv.com.

53. Quoted in Johnson, "Wake Up Call."

54. Quoted in Liz Goodwin, "New Research: Bullying Hurts Kids' Brains," *The Upshot* (blog), Yahoo! News, November 10, 2010. http://news.yahoo.com.

55. R. Douglas Fields, "Sticks and Stones—Hurtful Words Damage the Brain," *The New Brain* (blog), *Psychology Today,* October 30, 2010. www.psychologytoday.com.

56. Quoted in Sean Coughlan, "Childhood Bullying 'Damages Adult Life,'" BBC News, August 19, 2013. www.bbc.com.

Chapter Four: Ways to Stop the Bullying

57. Marlene Lutz, telephone interview with the author, December 29, 2014.

58. Quoted in "Obama: Bullying Shouldn't Be Inevitable, Accepted," NBC News.com, March 10, 2011, www.nbcnews.com.

59. Quoted in MassLive, "Obama Shocked, Saddened by Youth Suicides Linked to Bullying," October 22, 2010. www.masslive.com.

60. Liza, interview with the author, October 25, 2014.

61. Quoted in Michael Walsh, "Bullies Drench Autistic Boy in Bodily Fluids for Ice Bucket Challenge 'Prank,'" *New York Daily News,* September 4, 2014. www.nydailynews.com.

62. Facebook, "Facebook Community Standards." www.facebook.com.

63. Quoted in MouseMail, "More than 5 Million Children Under the Age of 10 at Risk," May 26, 2011. www.mousemail.com.

64. Quoted in Bazelon, *Sticks and Stones,* p. 266.

65. Quoted in Nick Bilton, "Meet Facebook's Mr. Nice," *New York Times,* October 22, 2014. www.nytimes.com.

66. Quoted in Bazelon, *Sticks and Stones,* p. 265.

67. Bazelon, *Sticks and Stones,* p. 265.

68. Quoted in Marlo Thomas, "In Their Own Words—16 Celebrities Who Survived Bullying," *Huffington Post,* August 4, 2013. www.huffingtonpost.com.

69. Quoted in Access Hollywood, "Lady Gaga Admits Being Bullied in High School Still Hurts: 'It Stays with You Your Whole Life,'" May 23, 2011. www.accesshollywood.com.

70. Quoted in Lydia Ann Stern, "Buddy Bench at Roundtown Elementary to Help Foster Friendships," *York Daily* (PA) *Record,* June 5, 2014. www.ydr.com.

71. Quoted in Chelsea Grainger, "Student Responds to Bullying with Positive Post-Its, School Punishes Her for Littering," *Toronto Sun*, October 7, 2014. www.torontosun.com.

72. Pete Reilly, interview with the author, December 2, 2014.

73. Quoted in *Campus Safety Magazine,* "Tackling School Bus Bullying," April 30, 2008. www.campussafetymagazine.com.

74. Quoted in *Campus Safety Magazine,* "Tackling School Bus Bullying."

75. Ellis, *We Want You to Know,* p. 115.

Cyberbullying Research Center (CRC)

5353 Parkside Dr.
Jupiter, FL 33458-2906
phone: (561) 799-8227
website: www.cyberbullying.us

The CRC is dedicated to providing current information about the nature, the causes, and the consequences of cyberbullying. The CRC's website contains a great deal of information for teachers, parents, and teens. Of special interest are cyberbullying victims' stories that can illustrate the dangers and the damage that can occur because of cyberbullying.

International Bullying Prevention Association (IBPA)

PO Box 99217
Troy, MI 48099
phone: (800) 929-0397
website: www.ibpaworld.org

The IBPA is a community dedicated to the prevention of bullying in all of its forms. Its website provides a list of books and articles that can help educators and parents understand bullying and also features webinars by experts in the field.

Peaceful Schools

506 Prospect Ave.
Syracuse, NY 13208
phone: (315) 558-4219
website: www.peacefulschools.com

This is an organization that works with schools to help them develop a community that engages students and staff by teaching them how to resolve conflicts through positive methods. The goal is to develop character and social skills and thereby reducing and preventing bullying and acts of violence.

Project Footsteps

1900 Hennepin Ave. South
Minneapolis, MN 55403
phone: (612) 353-6927
website: www.projectfootsteps.org

Project Footsteps works with students to change the culture of bullying. The organization helps schools establish action councils and teaches students how to address the bullying problems in their schools through websites, social media campaigns, and support for students who are victims of bullying.

STOMP Out Bullying

220 E. Fifty-Seventh St., 9th Floor, Suite G
New York, NY 10022-2820
phone: (877) 602-8559
website: www.stompoutbullying.org

This is a national antibullying and anti-cyberbullying organization for youth and teens. Its mission is to reduce cyberbullying and other types of harassment and to educate young people in how to address such problems.

PACER Center's Teens Against Bullying

8161 Normandale Blvd.
Bloomington, MN 55437
Phone: (800) 537-2237
website: www.pacerteensagainstbullying.org

PACER's website, created by and for teens, is a place for middle school and high school students to find ways to address bullying, to respond effectively, to share stories about bullying or being bullied, and to present ideas for ways that schools and communities can engage in solving the problem of bullying.

Books

Emily Bazelon, *Sticks and Stones: Defeating the Culture of Bullying and Rediscovering the Power of Character and Empathy.* New York: Random House, 2013.

Michael Carpenter and Robin D'Antona, *Bullying Solutions: Learn to Overcome from Real Case Studies.* Hauppauge, NY: Baron's Educational Series, 2014.

Sheryl Feinstein, *Secrets of the Teenage Brain.* New York: Skyhorse, 2013.

Gabrielle Ford with Sarah L. Thomson, *Gabe & Izzy: Standing Up for America's Bullied.* New York: Dial, 2014.

Raychelle Cassada Lohmann and Julia V. Taylor, *The Bullying Workbook for Teens: Activities to Help You Deal with Social Aggression and Cyberbullying.* Oakland, CA: New Harbinger, 2013.

Paula Todd, *Extreme Mean: Trolls, Bullies, and Predators Online.* Toronto: Signal, 2014.

Internet Sources

Nick Bilton, "Meet Facebook's Mr. Nice," *New York Times,* October 22, 2014. www.nytimes.com/2014/10/23/fashion/Facebook-Arturo-Bejar-Creating-Empathy-Among-Cyberbullying.html?_r=0.

David Dobbs, "Teenage Brains," *National Geographic,* October 2011. http://ngm.nationalgeographic.com/2011/10/teenage-brains/dobbs-text.

Matt Hamilton, "Father Fights Back Against Bullying After Son's Suicide," *Los Angeles Times,* October 19, 2013. http://

articles.latimes.com/2013/oct/19/nation/la-na-illinois-cyber
-bully-20131020.

Hara Estroff Marano, "Big Bad Bully," *Psychology Today,* April
12, 2013. www.psychologytoday.com/articles/200910/big-bad
-bully.

Websites

It Gets Better (www.itgetsbetter.org). Started by writer Dan
Savage and his partner, Terry Miller, as a way to stem the trend
of increased suicides by gay and questioning young people,
this website aims to give hope to LGBT youth suffering harassment. It features more than fifty thousand user-created videos
by a range of activists, celebrities, organizations, and politi-
cians that may help inspire and support visitors to the site.

Pacer's National Bullying Prevention (www.pacer.org/bully
ing). Founded in 2006, this site is dedicated to educating parents and young people that bullying is not an accepted rite
of passage. It offers resources for youth, teens, parents, and
teachers that can help break the cycle of bullying.

StopBullying.gov (www.stopbullying.gov). This site gives information about various types of bullying, who is at risk, and
ways to prevent it. There are helpful sections educating students about the role of bystanders in bullying and how to find
help for users who are being bullied currently.

Index

Note: Boldface page numbers indicate illustrations.

Picture Credits

Cover: Thinkstock Images

Depositphotos: 8, 46, 57

Thinkstock Images: 12, 26, 31, 40, 49

© Kevin Dodge/Blend Images/Corbis: 15

Associated Press: 21, 52, 62

© Biophoto Associates/Science Source: 35

Gail B. Stewart is the author of more than 180 books for children, teens, and young adults. She is the mother of three grown sons and lives with her husband in Minneapolis, Minnesota.